For Denise and Ben, for helping this book grow.

First published 2015 by Walker Books Ltd, 87 Vauxhall Walk, London
SE11 5HJ • 10 9 8 7 6 5 4 3 2 1 • Copyright © 2015 Michael Foreman
• The right of Michael Foreman to be identified as author/illustrator of
this work has been asserted by him in accordance with the Copyright,
Designs and Patents Act 1988 • This book has been typeset in Futura
• Printed in China • All rights reserved. No part of this book may be
reproduced, transmitted or stored in an information retrieval system
in any form or by any means, graphic, electronic or mechanical,
including photocopying, taping and recording, without prior written
permission from the publisher. • British Library Cataloguing in
Publication Data: a catalogue record for this book is available from the
British Library • ISBN 978-1-4063-5650-2 • **www.walker.co.uk**

# THE SEEDS of FRIENDSHIP

## MICHAEL FOREMAN

WALKER BOOKS
AND SUBSIDIARIES
LONDON · BOSTON · SYDNEY · AUCKLAND

# Adam loved his new home.

It was high, high in a tall tower in the city.

It was exciting. He was living in the sky.

But Adam missed
the faraway place
where he used to
live. Every evening
he asked his mum
and dad to read him
stories that brought
back memories of
their old home.

Adam drew pictures
to go with the stories
and pinned them on
his bedroom wall.

But when he looked from
his bedroom window, he
saw a very different picture.
He saw a cold, grey world.

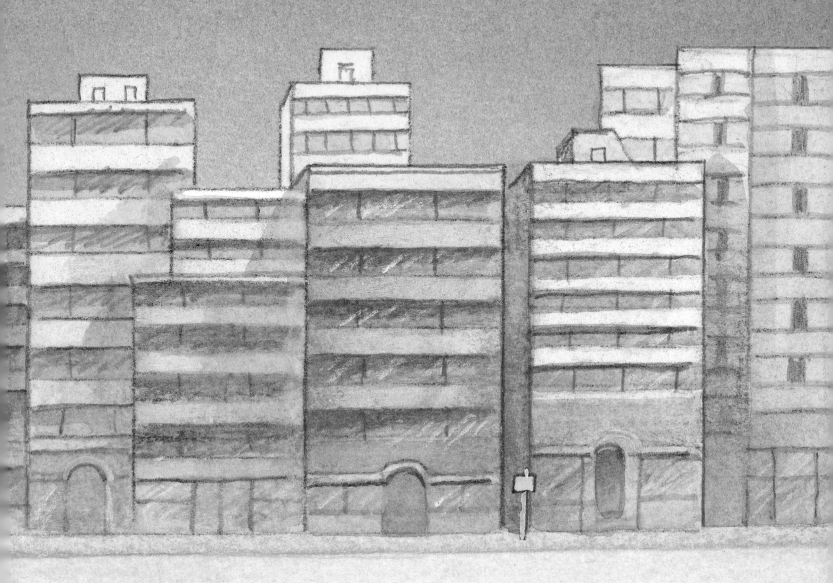

It seemed so empty, too.

Sometimes he saw children

playing far below in the shadows of the buildings,

but he was too shy to go down and say "hello".

Then one morning Adam couldn't see out of his window at all. The glass was frosted over and the icy patterns reminded Adam of a frozen forest.

With his finger, Adam drew animals to live there.

When his window-forest was full he ran to the next window, and the next, and the next, until every one was full.

That night Adam saw

snow for the first time.

In the morning, the dark, grey world was gone.

It was a white wonderland! Adam rushed

downstairs and out into the snow. It was so cold!

Some children were

building a snowman.

Adam touched the snow. It was light and wet and cold all at once. He started to build a snow elephant.

"That's a bit small for an elephant!" one of the children laughed. "Let's make a big one."

Then they threw a snowball at him.

Adam laughed.

So they all worked together to build

the biggest elephant that they could.

When they had finished, Adam started to make a snow hippo

and then a snow crocodile. The other children copied him

and soon there were snowy

rhinos, lions and a camel, too.

By supper time, the

snowman was in charge

of a whole snow-zoo!

A few days later, when the snowy world had melted, it was time for Adam to start at his new school.

He was pleased to see that some of his new friends were there. They showed him around. Adam's favourite place was a small garden. It was a wonderful splash of green in the grey playground.

Adam's teacher gave him some seeds from the
garden to take home. He gave them to his mum.
He didn't know what kind of seeds they were,
but Mum planted them in the window boxes.

"Let's see what happens," she said.

As the months passed, the school's garden grew and Adam brought more plants and seeds home. Once the window boxes were full, Adam and his friends found tin cans and pots and pans and carried them up to the roof. Together they made a garden in the sky.

"Let's make more gardens!" said the children.

So Adam and his friends made gardens on

any patch of waste ground they could find.

Now, Adam no longer sees a grey world.

He sees a city of gardens.

He knows that each season will bring

its own wonders and colours, and that

the seeds of friendship will never die.